I want to be a
SUPERMODEL

Katie Franks

PowerKiDS press.

New York

To Rachel, who loves supermodels

Published in 2007 by The Rosen Publishing Group, Inc.
29 East 21st Street, New York, NY 10010

First Edition

Editor: Jennifer Way
Book Design: Ginny Chu
Photo Researcher: Sam Cha

Photo Credits: All Photos © Getty Images.

Library of Congress Cataloging-in-Publication Data

Franks, Katie.
    I want to be a supermodel / Katie Franks. — 1st ed.
        p. cm. — (Dream jobs)
    Includes index.
    ISBN-13: 978-1-4042-3620-2 (library binding)
    ISBN-10: 1-4042-3620-1 (library binding)
    1. Models (Persons)—Vocational guidance—Juvenile literature.
    I. Title.
    HD8039.M77F73 2007
    746.9'2023—dc22
                                                    2006019462

Manufactured in the United States of America

Contents

Tyra Banks is a supermodel who has gone on to present the TV show *America's Next Top Model*.

Supermodels

What do you think of when you hear the word "supermodel?" You may picture the models who appear in **magazines** and on TV. You might think about famous models who get to travel the world to work on **fashion** shows. You might wonder how a model becomes known as a supermodel. This book will show you some of the things that all models do and what makes supermodels special.

One of the biggest supermodels in the 1990s was Elle MacPherson.

The Supermodel Era

The 1980s and 1990s were known as the supermodel **era**. This is because so many supermodels became famous during this period. A few examples of these supermodels are Linda Evangelista, Naomi Campbell, Christy Turlington, Elle MacPherson, Cindy Crawford, and Claudia Schiffer. They were some of the highest-paid and most famous women in the world. They appeared in fashion runway shows and on the covers of lots of magazines.

Kate Moss is an example of a short supermodel. She is only 5 feet 7 inches (1.7 m) tall. However, she is one of the world's most famous models.

What It Takes

Very few people can become models because of the **physical** requirements. Models must be tall, have a thin body, and have an interesting face. The height for female models is generally at least 5 feet 9 inches (1.8 m). Models must fit these requirements because the clothes used in fashion shows come in certain sizes, so only the people who will fit into the clothes can model them.

Gisele Bundchen is signed with IMG Model Management.

Modeling Agencies

One of the first things a supermodel does in her **career** is get signed by a modeling **agency**. Agencies help models find work by sending them to meet **clients**. This meeting is called a casting call. When the client chooses a model, she is said to have booked the job. Early in their careers, models do not book many jobs. As they become more known, they book more, higher-paying, and more fun jobs.

Both models and actresses like to wear the clothes of designer Zac Posen.

Fun with Fashion

One of the fun things supermodels get to do is work with famous fashion **designers**. Many fashion designers have supermodels with whom they like to work. They use them in their fashion shows and for **advertising** for their clothes. Many supermodels have become seen as part of a designer's **image**. For example, Naomi Campbell worked for a long time with Versace.

Naomi Campbell has walked the runway in many fashion shows.

Walking the Runway

Another thing that supermodels do is work fashion shows. Designers hold them to show off their work. Fashion shows are held several times a year in cities around the world. Some of these cities are New York City, Paris, France, and Milan, Italy. Supermodels show the designer's clothes on the runway in front of an **audience**. The people at the show are sometimes famous actors, as well as people who work for fashion magazines.

Heidi Klum has appeared on many magazine covers. Here she is showing the cover she did for *Elle* magazine.

Magazine Covers

Supermodels are known for being on lots of magazine covers. For example, Gisele Bundchen has appeared on more than 200 magazine covers! Being on the cover of a magazine is an important marker of a supermodel's career. It means that the magazine that puts her on the cover thinks that she will help sell the magazine. It also helps make her more famous and helps her get more money for other jobs.

Adriana Lima has done advertising campaigns for Maybelline, GUESS?, and Victoria's Secret.

Advertising Campaigns

Supermodels are often used in big advertising **campaigns**. This is because their fame can help sell **products**. If an advertising campaign lasts a long time, people often start to think of a supermodel as the "face" of the product. This can help both the model and the product become more well-known. For example, Kate Moss was the face of Calvin Klein for many years.

Petra Nemcova has worked to help the people who lived through the 2004 tsunami in Asia. A tsunami is a big storm that starts over the ocean.

Charity Work

In their free time, many supermodels like to do **charity** work. They hope that their fame can help bring people's attention to causes that are important to them. This can bring in more money and people to help those causes. Supermodels have helped charities that help people who suffer from illnesses and groups that help people who have lived through natural **disasters**.

Branching Out

Some supermodels work in other fields after they have modeled for a while. Many have become singers or actors. Rebecca Romijn and Milla Jovovich have both appeared in several movies. Others have gone on to present TV shows. You might watch Tyra Banks on *America's Next Top Model* or Heidi Klum on *Project Runway*. Models who can branch out and find work beyond the runway have longer careers and are almost always known as supermodels.

Glossary

advertising (AD-vur-tyz-ing) Telling people about a product or something a person needs.

agency (AY-jen-see) A company that helps models find work.

audience (AH-dee-ints) A group of people who watch or listen to something.

campaigns (kam-PAYNZ) Plans to get certain results.

career (kuh-REER) A job.

charity (CHER-uh-tee) A group that gives help to the needy.

clients (KLY-ents) People who pay a company or other people to do something.

designers (dih-ZY-nurz) People who make plans for clothes.

disasters (dih-ZAS-terz) Things that cause suffering or loss.

era (ER-uh) A period of time or history.

fashion (FA-shun) The latest clothes.

image (IH-mij) The public face of a brand.

magazines (MA-guh-zeenz) A weekly or monthly grouping of pictures and articles.

physical (FIH-zih-kul) Having to do with the body.

products (PRAH-dukts) Things that are produced.

Index

Web Sites

Due to the changing nature of Internet links, PowerKids Press has developed an online list of Web sites related to the subject of this book. This site is updated regularly. Please use this link to access the list:

www.powerkidslinks.com/djobs/supermod/